LOST IN THE FOG

by Irving Bacheller   adapted and illustrated by Loretta Krupinski

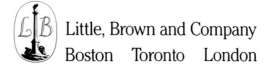

Little, Brown and Company

Boston   Toronto   London

To my daughter, Jennifer, who helps to keep the child in me alive—L. K.

Library of Congress Cataloging-in-Publication Data

Krupinski, Loretta.
     Lost in the fog / by Irving Bacheller; adapted and illustrated by
Loretta Krupinski.
          p.   cm.
     Summary: When a thick fog surrounds their rowboat, a boy and an
old woman are rescued by the very geese they are taking to market.

     ISBN 0-316-07462-4
     [1. Geese — Fiction.   2. Fog — Fiction.]   I. Bacheller, Irving,
1859 – 1950.   Lost in the fog.   II. Title.
PZ7.K94624Lo 1990
[E] — dc19   88-25923
                                                                         CIP
                                                                          AC

          10   9   8   7   6   5   4   3   2   1

                              SC
          Published simultaneously in Canada
     by Little, Brown & Company (Canada) Limited

                    Printed in Hong Kong

As a boy I never could understand how anyone could ever have any love for a goose. For when I first appeared in the glory of my new long pants, a wild flock of geese came rushing after me. Tweaking and hissing and screaming, they pulled me down and pecked me unmercifully. After that, I treasured a most unrighteous hatred of the whole goose family. They were to me a low, waddling tribe with the evil spirit of envy in them.

Mother Tipton lived in a shanty all by herself on a little bit of land known as Mother Tipton's Hollow. I used to think the worst thing about her was her geese. Reserves of them covered the green slopes of the Hollow, and as a white squadron they sailed the black waters of the pond in its center. Whenever I came visiting of a summer day and fearfully peered over the ridge, a stir of white wings and a yell of defiance greeted me. Yet Mother Tipton herself was a kindly woman who rescued me whenever I was captured by that noisy rabble of boy-haters.

The Hollow was not far from the shore of the broad Sound. Mother Tipton often took her geese and feathers to market in a rowboat, and she rowed as strong an oar as any man of all the many that made their living on those waters.

One morning—I was then a boy of eight years—I got permission to go with her. She had a cargo of ten young geese, which were stowed away, their legs tied together, in the bow of the boat.

It was a mile and a half across the bay, and the water lay like a millpond, with scarcely a ripple showing. A thin mist hovered about the farther shore as we pulled away, but we could see the dock clearly and the building that lay beyond it.

"Land o' Goshen!" Mother Tipton cried, after rowing a few minutes. "It's foggin'." Then she sat a long time, looking over the water at a misty wall that lay not far ahead of us. Suddenly she began to pull vigorously on the right oar.

"It's the ebb tide," said she, "and we must get back as quick as we can, or we'll be in trouble."

The fog thickened fast, and presently the boat had seemed to lengthen and we seemed to go far apart, so that I could only dimly see the face of Mother Tipton. Then I heard her groan and breathe heavily as she put all her strength to the oars. She was lifting the bow from the water every stroke now. Then, suddenly, I heard the snap of an oar, the boat turned in the tide, and a splash of water hit my face.

Mother Tipton rose in the boat and shouted a long halloo. We listened for some answer, but, hearing none, she called "Help!" a dozen times, at the top of her voice. Between her cries we could hear nothing but the tide rippling under the boat, pulling us out into the bay.

Having little sense at best, and none of our danger, I felt a thrill of adventure then. Mother Tipton started crying in her seat, and I bravely did my best to comfort her.

She was soon up shouting for help again, but not a sound came back to us. We drifted with the tide and could see nothing. Mother Tipton kept calling all the time, but my tongue was dry for the need of water, and I lost a bit of my bravery. It was time to be getting home — there was no longer any doubt of that.

"Mother Tipton," I said, "where do you suppose we are?"

"The Lord only knows, child," was her answer. "I'm afraid we're out in the deep water half over to Long Island. But the tide has turned, and it may take us back before night comes. We'll just sit still and keep calling."

I was leaning over the side of the boat and feeling miserable when I heard a great disturbance among the geese.

"Willie, come here," said Mother Tipton. Two of the geese were lying in her lap, and she was unwinding a long fish-line.

"Tie it tightly," said she, "just above the big joint of the leg. Wait — let's cut it first into even lengths. That's right — now cut it."

She measured for me, and I cut the line, as she held it, into ten pieces. Then we tied them securely to the geese. Next, we fastened the loose ends together, winding them with a bit of string. We tied another fish-line to this ten-stranded cable, cut the geese apart, and let them all go at once.

They flew for a little distance, but, not being all of a mind, they came down in a rather bad tangle. I kept hold of the line as they ducked their heads in the water, shook their wings, and screamed as if delighted with their liberty. Then they began to pull like a team of horses, and I could feel the stretch of the line. Suddenly, still clutching the line, I went overboard! There was a thunder of wings when the geese saw me coming after them.

I knew I must not let go of the line, and they began to pull me through the water at a great rate. I was a good swimmer, but I lay over on my back and was dragged along. Then I heard the voice of Mother Tipton calling me. I looked in the direction it came from, and I got a scare I hope never to have again. I could see nothing of the boat.

The fog lay on the sea as thick as darkness, and I was alone and frightened. Breathing hard, trying not to panic, I lay for a long time floating on my back, my fingers clutching the tight strings.

Then I turned over and got a little of the water out of my eyes. I heard, faintly, the voice of Mother Tipton in the distance calling the geese, just as I had heard her many a time in the Hollow. The geese turned and listened, and then the whole flock veered about, cackling together as if they knew the meaning of Mother Tipton's call. The ten of them were now swimming comfortably. Every moment I could hear more distinctly Mother Tipton's voice, and, after a short while, I could hear the water on the boat. Suddenly, its bow broke through the wall of fog, and I saw my companion looming above me in the thick air. I called to her, she greeted us with a cheery "Thank Heaven!" and the whole flock rose out of the water and tried to fly.

The geese came up to the boat side, and she touched their beaks fondly with her hand as she came to help me in. The water had chilled me through. I was glad to set my feet on the boat bottom and to take off my coat and wrap my shoulders in the warm shawl that Mother Tipton offered. You may be sure I kept a good hold of the strings, and before I sat down we tied them fast to some ten feet of the small anchor rope and tied it at the bow.

At first, the geese lay quietly under the gunwale, as Mother Tipton fussed with them. She shooed them off in a moment, and they made away, turning their heads knowingly as she began to paddle.

"I believe those creatures will have sense enough to go ashore. They know more than we do about a good many things," said she. "That old gander of mine goes a mile away sometimes, but he gets home, even if it *is* foggy, every night of his life."

It was growing dark, and in five minutes we couldn't. see our team. I was kneeling in the bow, my hand on the rope, peering to get a view of the geese, when I heard a loud quacking and a big ripple in the water just ahead. I was about to speak, when I saw a group of dark objects on either side of the boat. I made out what they were and caught one of them by the neck just as Mother Tipton shouted "Ducks! Ducks stay close to shore!"

It was not long before we heard our boat bottom grinding on the sand, but it was very dark. Mother Tipton went to the bow of the boat, and I was near the middle seat.

"Thank Heaven, we're somewhere!" I heard her say, and then she stood up. I heard her paddle strike in the sand and felt the boat lift forward and go up on the dry beach. I was out pulling in a moment, and I tell you the firm earth had never so good a feeling. I felt my way up the beach, and Mother Tipton came after me. It was so dark and foggy we could see nothing. After a little, I felt the grass under me, and my companion lit a match and touched it to a bit of paper she had taken off a bundle in the boat.

"Make haste, now," she said, "and pick up all the bits of small wood you see around."

The dry driftwood lay all around us, and in half a minute a good bit of it was crackling on that flaming wad of paper. We brought sticks as thick as a man's leg and fed the flames until they leapt higher than our heads and lit the misty reaches of the shore a good distance.

"Lawsy me!" said she, presently. "I think we're on Charles Island." Then she took a brand out of the fire and, waving it above her head, walked away in the thick grass. She called to me in a moment.

"Bring the fish-line and the tin pail!"

I went to the boat for them and was shortly groping through the tall grass in the direction of that flickering torch.

I found her by an old ruin of a house, peering into a deep well. We were not long tying that line to the pail and dropping it down the well hole. The line raced through my fingers, and the pail bounded as it struck and rang like a bell on the splashing water. When I had hauled it up, we sat looking at the golden flare of the torch shining on the slopping cylinder of cold, clear water.

She took the pail, buried her mouth at the rim, and nearly smothered herself with the water. I thanked her mightily when I got my hands on it, for I had a fever of thirst in me. When my dry tongue was soaking in the sweet, pure water, I could feel my heart lighten.

"Now let's take a pailful with us and get supper," said Mother Tipton. "We're on Charles Island, five miles from home, but it isn't more than half a mile from Milford. We'd better stop here for the night, and maybe it'll be clear before morning."

I took the torch, and she dragged behind her a bit of the fallen roof that had once covered the old house. By the light of the fire we began to dig clams with the oar and paddle. In ten minutes we had enough for a fine bake. Laying them out on a rock, we raked the hot coals over them. When they were ready, we ate the clams, and, while some butter would have helped a bit, they tasted fine.

After supper we untied the flock, set it free, and dragged the boat above the tidewater. Then we drove two stakes in front of a rock near the fire and set our strip of roofing over it all. Under it we threw a good layer of hot sand from near the fire and built high ridges on either side of our shelter. There were sacks of down for pillows, and my overcoat and the big woolen shawl as covering. The warm sand gave me a grateful sense of comfort. I lay for a time and looked at the dying firelight, but before very long I fell asleep.

As I awoke the next day, I could hear the bellow of a great fog siren, sending its echoes crashing through the dungeon of mist. Next I noticed the sound of the noisy water on the rocks nearby. It was growing light, and somebody was poking the fire. When I lifted my head, I felt a warm breeze and saw the fog had gone.

A man with a wooden leg and a patch of gray whiskers was standing by the fire.

I crept out and greeted him, rubbing my eyes with drowsiness.

"Ketched in the fog, I suppose," said he, kicking the fire.

"Yes, sir," I answered. "We were caught by the tide and lost, yesterday."

"Hum!" he muttered, as he glanced under the lean-to roof of our shanty and took a good look at Mother Tipton. "Rather a tidy bit of a woman — stout as an ox an' a good-looker."

"Don't disturb her," I said.

"Not for the world," he answered, returning and shying another bit of wood at the fire. "I like t' see 'em sleep — it's good for 'em. Got anything for breakfus'?"

"I'm going to dig some clams," I answered.

"You jes' wait," he said, winking at me, "an' I'll go off to the boat an' bring ye some coffee an' fish an' bread an' butter. Got loads of it aboard there. No trouble at all."

He made off for a small rowboat that lay on the beach nearby, then rowed off around the point. I walked down the shore a few yards and, from a high rock, saw a boat lying at anchor a little way offshore. By the time the man came back, bringing a basket of provisions, Mother Tipton was up, and I had a good fire going.

"Madam," he said, laying down the basket, "may I be so bold as to offer you su'thin' for your breakfus'? Here's a snack o' coffee an' fish an' a tidy bit o' bread an' butter."

She thanked him, and while we were eating breakfast he told us that he was a menhaden-fisherman "— as owned his own boat." Then we told him our story. Afterward, he insisted on taking us home.

We were glad to accept his kindness, and the sun was shining brightly when we put off for the tug with all our geese in the boat. I made Mother Tipton promise that not one of them would ever be turned into soup. The captain brought a big armchair and made Mother Tipton very comfortable in the bow of the boat. We were home in an hour, and I was as glad to get there as all were to see me.

The adventure resulted in great good, for it gave me some respect for geese and gave Mother Tipton a great respect for the sailor. It was not long after that she added to her house in the Hollow a man with a wooden leg. You may be sure I went to the wedding.